Spotlight on Cody

Also by Betsy Duffey

Spotlight on Cody

Betsy Duffey

Illustrated by Ellen Thompson

Viking

VIKING
Published by the Penguin Group
Penguin Putnam Books for Young Readers, 345 Hudson Street, New York,
New York 10014, U.S.A.
Penguin Books Ltd, 27 Wrights Lane, London W8 5TZ, England
Penguin Books Australia Ltd, Ringwood, Victoria, Australia
Penguin Books Canada Ltd, 10 Alcorn Avenue, Toronto, Ontario,
Canada M4V 3B2
Penguin Books (N.Z.) Ltd, 182-190 Wairau Road, Auckland 10, New Zealand

Penguin Books Ltd, Registered Offices: Harmondsworth, Middlesex, England

First published in 1998 by Viking, a member of Penguin Putnam Inc.

1 3 5 7 9 10 8 6 4 2

Text copyright © Betsy Duffey, 1998
Illustrations copyright © Ellen Thompson, 1998
All rights reserved

LIBRARY OF CONGRESS CATALOGING-IN-PUBLICATION DATA
Duffey, Betsy.
Spotlight on Cody / Betsy Duffey ; illustrated by Ellen Thompson.   p.   cm.
Summary: Nine-year-old Cody Michaels is bound for stardom in the
third grade talent show just as soon as he figures out his talent.
ISBN 0-670-88077-9
[1. Talent shows—Fiction. 2. Schools—Fiction.]
I. Thompson, Ellen (Ellen M.), ill. II. Title.
PZ7.D876Sp 1998 [Fic]—DC21   98-17461 CIP AC

Printed in U.S.A.
Set in Plantin

Contents

Chapter 1

The Amazing Untalented Boy

"I think he's dead," Cody said.

Cody, Chip, P.J., and Holly stood at the back table of the classroom, staring down into a small jar. Inside was a tiny gray caterpillar that they had just named Joe. Joe was not moving.

"Ms. Harvey!" P.J. waved her arm in the air. "If our caterpillar dies, do we get points off of our grade?"

Ms. Harvey looked up from her desk. "Class," she said, "it's normal for the caterpillars to be immobile. After all, they just flew all the way here from California in a box. They are just resting."

"He's gross," P.J. said.

"I think he's cute," Holly said. Cody looked up and smiled at Holly. There was something so cool about a girl who liked bugs.

"I just wish he would do something," P.J. said. "What are we going to write about in our science log books if he's dead?"

Cody drew the jar. Then he drew Joe lying on the bottom of the jar and labeled the picture. It looked great.

"Finish up on your log books," Ms. Harvey called out. "When you're done, get back to your seats. I have a surprise for you." She sounded excited. Cody closed his book.

Everyone hurried back to their seats and looked at Ms. Harvey. "We are going to put on a talent show!" she said. "It will be next Friday night. That gives us two weeks to get ready."

Everyone began talking at once.

"Cool!" said Chip.

"I'll sing!" P.J. said. "Laaaaaaaaaaa!" she sang out, like an opera singer. Chip and Cody covered their ears and made faces at each other.

"Settle down everyone," Ms. Harvey said. "If you want to share, raise your hand."

Hands waved wildly.

Cody sat back. A talent show. Great! Maybe *he* should do a singing act. The announcer would say, "We now present the Amazing Talented Boy." Cody would step out wearing a cool, wild, shiny shirt and dark sunglasses. Only he wouldn't be an opera singer, he'd be a rock star, singing into a sparkly silver microphone. His pencil became a mike.

"Oooo, baby, baby."

"Cody, raise your hand if you have something to share with the class." Ms. Harvey tapped her foot. Cody slapped his hand over his mouth.

P.J. giggled.

Holly smiled at him and winked. He sighed. There was something so cool about a girl who winked and smiled, especially at him.

The singing act was a good idea. There was only one thing wrong. He couldn't sing.

"I'll probably play the trumpet," Chip said.

The trumpet. Playing a musical instrument was cool, but not the trumpet . . . the drums. "We now present the Amazing Talented Boy." He played a few taps with his pencils. Soft at first then faster and faster and . . . Cody hit an imaginary cymbal with one pencil. The drumstick flew across the room.

"Cody's throwing pencils!" P.J. said.

Ms. Harvey's face was red. "Cody Michaels, did you throw that pencil?"

P.J. giggled again.

"Sorry," he said. "It was an accident." Ms. Harvey frowned.

Drums would be perfect. There was only one thing wrong. He couldn't play the drums.

He looked around the room. The other kids were smiling and seemed very excited about the talent show.

"What are you going to do?" Chip whispered to him.

He didn't answer.

He opened his log book and looked at the picture of Joe lying at the bottom of the jar. Everyone was watching Joe, waiting for him to do something. But what? He knew just how Joe felt.

"I'll do a magic act," said Doug.

"I'm going to make a video," said Holly.

Cody imagined the classroom as a three-ring circus. In each ring kids were singing or dancing or playing musical instruments.

Then the ringmaster stepped up to the mike. "Ladies and gentlemen . . ."

Cody sank lower in his seat.

"We now present to you . . ."

Cody closed his eyes.

"The Amazing Untalented Boy!"

In his mind the circus ring shrank until it was exactly the size of the bottom of Joe's jar.

My Science Log: The Life of Joe

Jar

Joe

Day One: Morning
Joe arrived today. Soon he will begin to move and eat. I hope.

Chapter 2

"Run for It!"

Cody sat with Chip in the lunchroom. At the table next to them P.J. was singing into her corn dog. "My country, 'tis of thee . . ."

Doug was making French fries disappear at the end of the table.

Angel danced by with her lunch tray.

Cody was still.

All the other kids had talent. He tried to think of something that he could do for the show that didn't require any talent.

Cody had seen a man in the park last Saturday. The man hadn't spoken. He had just acted out things without words, like being

8

surprised, and getting trapped in a box, and pulling an imaginary rope. A mime.

Maybe he could do that! It didn't even require talking.

Cody pretended to be surprised. He opened his eyes wide. He opened his mouth wide. He threw his hands into the air. A first grader dropped his tray and ran for his teacher.

Cody put his hands down quickly. His stomach growled.

Maybe he would try to act out being hungry. He waved to get the other kids' attention. He tried to look sad. He pointed to his mouth.

"Ms. Brush," Angel called out to the lunchroom teacher. "Cody's sick. He's about to throw up."

Ms. Brush rushed across the cafeteria toward him.

"Ewwwwwww," P.J. said.

"Cody's gonna barf," another kid called out.

"Run for it!" Doug said.

The kids at his table started grabbing their trays and getting up.

"I'm okay," Cody called out. "I promise!" Ms. Brush moved away, and the kids sat back down. Cody ruled out being a mime.

"What do people who don't have any talent do?" he asked Chip.

Chip slurped the last of his chocolate milk as he thought. "Everybody has a talent," he said.

"But what if someone didn't?"

"My mother says that in the Miss America pageant if someone doesn't have a talent they do a reading."

"What's a reading?" Cody asked.

"You pick out a poem or a story that you like and read it or act it out."

Cody thought for a minute. He had seen a man do that on TV once. The man had held a skull. "To be or not to be. That is the question," the man had said.

Cody could do that. But he wouldn't read

anybody else's stuff. That seemed wrong, like using someone else's homework.

He would write his own poem and recite it. He would write a terrific poem.

He could imagine the cheers, the applause, the spotlight.

Where could he get a skull? Maybe he could use the poem he had written for Valentine's Day.

I Love My Computer
Roses are red,
Pickles are green,
What I love most
Is my computer screen.

It wasn't quite right.

He thought about his poem all through lunch, and when he got back to the class-room, he took out a fresh sheet of paper. He would write about something that would make people laugh, and cry, and most of all applaud. He would write about his dog, Pal.

What rhymes with dog, he wondered. Hog. Bog. Log. Polliwog.

That should be enough.

> *Pal is a dog.*
> *He is not a hog.*
> *He does not live in a bog*
> *or lie on a log*
> *or eat a polliwog.*

He put his hand on his heart like the man with the skull. He imagined reading the poem: "Pal is a dog. . . ." It didn't seem right. It might make people laugh, but not cry and applaud. He made a face. He ruled out reading.

"Hey," Chip called out from the back of the room. "Joe is eating!" Everyone rushed to the science table. The little gray caterpillars were all moving around the bottom of their jars eating leaves. Everyone was so proud.

Cody looked at Joe eating happily in the jar

while sounds of praise echoed around him.

For some reason it reminded Cody of kindergarten. No matter what you did in kindergarten, everyone thought it was a big deal. The encouraging words of Mrs. Willaman, his kindergarten teacher, came back to him:

"You pasted this? Way to go, Cody!"

"You put on your coat? Way to go, Cody!"

"You washed your hands? Way to go, Cody!"

He wished it could still be like that—doing simple, ordinary things and being praised for them.

He looked down at Joe and whispered, "Don't grow up."

My Science Log: The Life of Joe

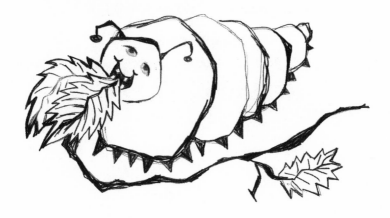

Day One: Afternoon
Joe is eating! Way to go, Joe!

Chapter 3

Cody hurried into the house after school.
When he heard music he remembered that his
mother had taken the day off from work. It
was his father's birthday, and she had planned
a special dinner.

"Mom?" he called.

Cody's mother was stepping up and down
on a pink plastic step in time to the music.

"One, two," she said between deep breaths.

"Mom?"

"Uh huh?" she said. She never stopped
stepping up and down on the step.

Cody sat on the sofa and watched her. "There's a talent show at school next week. Has anyone in our family ever had a talent?"

She didn't answer right away. Her eyes were focused on the TV. On the screen, a woman in a purple leotard was kicking her foot forward as she stepped up on a step.

Cody's mother kicked like the woman on TV. Cody blinked.

"Your uncle Mike could yodel," she said finally. "I think he won a yodeling contest when he was about your age."

Yodel?

Cody pictured himself at the talent show in those little leather shorts and suspenders that yodelers wear, and a little green cap like Peter Pan.

Yikes! A guy could get beat up for wearing an outfit like that!

He needed a talent that would not require any funny clothes.

"Any other talents?"

"Hmmm," she said. She was now swinging both arms forward like she was going to jump off a diving board, but she stepped back down each time instead.

"Your aunt Dot could clog."

Clog?

It sounded like something bad that happens to plumbing.

"What's clog?" Cody asked.

"It's a dance," she said. "A kind of country dance."

He could imagine the announcer at the talent show. "Cody Michaels will now clog."

He needed a talent that didn't make it sound like he was about to do something gross.

"Any others?" he asked hopefully.

"My mother could do a split."

Cody tried to imagine his grandmother doing a split. He couldn't. He thought about doing a split himself.

Ouch! He would need a less painful talent.

"Anything else?"

Well, your dad juggles. Or at least he used to be able to juggle."

"Juggle?" Now Cody was interested.

Juggling would be a great talent. It didn't require a costume. It didn't sound gross. It wouldn't be painful. He imagined the announcer saying, "Ladies and gentlemen. Cody Michaels will now juggle."

It would be perfect.

"Does he still have any of his juggling stuff?" Cody asked his mother.

His mother didn't answer for a moment. She was kicking her back leg out when she stepped up, and it seemed to require a lot of concentration.

"He didn't have anything special," she said finally. "He just juggled ordinary things. Tennis balls. Apples and oranges. And eggs."

Eggs!

Cody was suddenly so excited he could hardly breathe.

The curtain would open. He would slowly pull three eggs from a basket and show them to the crowd.

"*Ooooooo!*" He could imagine the looks on people's faces when he showed them the eggs. Then he would begin. The eggs would fly up into the air, moving gracefully between his hands. Higher and higher he would juggle them.

But could he learn to juggle in two weeks?

Juggling looked easy. You just tossed things up into the air and caught them. All he needed was three eggs and a little practice.

"Mom?" he asked.

"Yeah?" She was pushing her arms up like a cheerleader with pompoms.

"Can I practice for the talent show?"

"Sure, honey."

He turned to go into the kitchen.

"Oh Cody," she called out. "Don't touch that coconut cake. It's for your dad's birthday dinner."

"I won't," he said.

He knew just what he needed, and it wasn't a coconut cake. It was right in the refrigerator in a small white carton.

He stopped in front of the refrigerator and said in an announcer's voice, "Cody Michaels will now juggle."

Chapter 4

The Amazing Juggling Boy

Cody stretched his fingers and popped his knuckles.

His dog, Pal, lay asleep beside the refrigerator.

"Pal," he said to the dog. "You are about to witness the Amazing Juggling Boy."

Cody opened the refrigerator and checked the eggs. There were twelve. He smiled. He only needed three.

He picked up one of the eggs. It was cold in his hand.

He looked at the coconut cake on the counter. For an egg to reach the cake it would have to go all the way over the sink and past the toaster. He would be careful.

"Introducing Cody Michaels, world-famous juggler," he said to Pal in a deep voice. Pal thumped his tail. "The world-famous juggler will now juggle one egg!" He held the egg up to show Pal.

Pal didn't open his eyes. It would work better with a real audience.

With one hand, he tossed the egg up about five inches. It landed back in his other hand with a soft plop.

"Ta daaa!" he said.

He bowed. "Thank you. Thank you," he said.

Juggling was going to be a cinch. He had found his talent.

He looked at the egg in his hand. Time to be more daring. He tossed the egg high into the air, but this time it wasn't going straight up. Cody lunged forward to catch it.

Plop! Safe in his hand.

Whew! He let out a breath. That was close,

but he had shown his true skill. He had mastered one egg.

"Ta daaa!"

Time for two.

He took another egg out of the carton. Now he had one in each hand. He would toss them up and catch each egg in the other hand. He took a deep breath. He tossed them up a little and . . .

Plop, plop. He caught them!

"Ta daaaa!"

Cody got out the third egg. Now he held two eggs in one hand and one egg in the other. "The Amazing Juggling Boy," he said in the deep voice, "will now juggle *three* eggs." He held them up for Pal.

Cody concentrated. He made a tossing motion with his hands, but he did not let go of the eggs.

He closed his eyes and imagined himself at the talent show. The spotlight would be on him alone. The kids would be cheering.

"One," he said.

"Two."

"Three."

He tossed all three eggs into the air at once.

The eggs rose in slow motion. He watched them gliding up. He saw them falling down. He saw his hands desperately grabbing in all directions. The amazing juggling hands that had helped him only moments before now let him down.

The first egg smacked onto the clean kitchen floor. The second egg hit the coffeepot on the counter. But the third egg kept sailing farther, much farther. Over the sink, beyond the toaster . . .

"No!" Cody yelled as he lunged for the egg. Too late. It hit with a splat. Dead center. Coconut flew in all directions as the egg broke and yolk dripped down the sides of the cake.

His mouth fell open.

Behind him in the doorway he heard his mother gasp.

This time, he did not say "Ta daaaa!"

Chapter 5

Smile Lines

Cody stood at the top of the stairs and listened to his parents talking below.

His mother had scraped all the coconut icing off of the cake and made a new batch. She had also grounded him for the rest of the week. Now he was trying to hear if they were talking about him.

He peeked down the staircase and saw his father leaning toward the hall mirror. "There," his father was saying, "a gray hair. No, two! Two gray hairs. I'm getting old. A fool at forty is a fool indeed."

Cody's father liked to talk in sayings.

"Come away from that mirror," his mother said.

"And wrinkles!" his dad said. "Look right there." He pointed to the corner of his eye.

"That's a smile line," Cody's mother said. Cody wondered what a smile line was.

"Look. Here's the mail," his mother said. "This will take your mind off gray hair and wrinkles. Look how many birthday cards came for you today." She sounded like she was in a better mood now. It was safe to come down.

Cody came downstairs and gave his dad a hug. "Happy birthday," he said.

"Thanks," his dad said as he hugged Cody back.

His father flipped through the pile of envelopes. "Look at all these cards." He fanned them out. "Maybe turning forty isn't so bad." He opened the first one. Cody sat beside him and looked at the cover.

"*Wine improves with age. Cheese improves*

with age," Cody's father read aloud.

He opened the card and read inside. "*Too bad you're not wine or cheese.*"

Cody's mother laughed. Cody's father frowned and put the card down. "Your aunt Sue has a sick sense of humor," he said to Cody.

"Let's see what Grandma sent," Cody said as he picked up one postmarked Topeka. He shook it to see if she had sent money. No cash. He handed the card to his father.

"*You know you're getting old . . .*" his father read, "*when your wrinkles get wrinkles.*"

Cody's father put the card down. "My own mother!" he said sadly.

Cody's mother laughed. "Read more, read more," she said.

His father was feeling his face. "Do my wrinkles have wrinkles?" he asked. He got up from the sofa. "I've had about all the fun I can stand," he said. He looked unhappy. "I just want to get this birthday over with."

"Hon-ey," Cody's mother said. "They're

just joking. That's their way of telling you how much they love you."

"Why don't they just come over and hit me with hammers?"

"Sit back down," his mother said. "I'm going to put the finishing touches on your birthday dinner." She left for the kitchen.

His father sat back down and stared at the little piles of cards.

"Sticks and stones can break my bones," he said, "but words can never hurt me."

Cody thought back to his last birthday—the candles on the cake, the kids singing "Happy Birthday." It had been a happy day.

Then he thought about his grandmother's birthday. She had just turned eighty years old. She was very happy. When did birthdays become something to dread instead of something to celebrate? And when did they change back to something to celebrate?

His dad put the cards down and looked at Cody. "I hear you had a little juggling problem today," he said.

Cody nodded and looked down at his shoes. "We're having a talent show at school," he said. "How did you learn to juggle?"

"Practice makes perfect," his dad said.

"Will you teach me?"

"Sure." His dad looked at the fruit bowl on the coffee table. He picked up a wooden orange. "I started with one thing." he said.

He tossed the orange up and caught it.

"I can do that," Cody said. He picked up an orange and tossed it up and caught it.

"Good," his dad said. "Do that over and over for a few days. Next week we'll add another orange."

Next week? Cody sighed. Next week would be too late.

Cody tossed the orange up. He caught it.

He tossed it again and caught it. He could suddenly see himself on stage.

Cody Michaels will now juggle one orange.

He would toss it up and he would catch it.

He would toss it again and he would catch

it. Catching one orange was not a talent. He put the orange back in the bowl.

"Maybe juggling isn't your thing," his dad said.

"What else can I do for the talent show?"

"Well, think of your best thing and do it."

"Dinner!" his mom called from the kitchen.

Cody's dad sighed. "Let's go get this over with," he said. He sounded like he was talking about a trip to the dentist or taking a test—or maybe even about being in a talent show.

Cody followed his dad into the kitchen. So far he had ruled out singing, playing the drums, miming, dramatic reading, yodeling, clogging, splitting, and juggling. Was there anything left?

All day Tuesday he tried to think of his best thing.

Nothing.

All day Wednesday he tried to think of his best thing.

Nothing.

Did he have a best thing?

My Science Log: The Life of Joe

Day Two:
Joe keeps eating and eating. Is eating a talent?

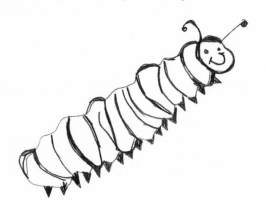

Day Three:
Joe has really grown. Is growing a talent?

Chapter 6

Sticks and Stones

On Thursday, Ms. Harvey came in carrying a big banner. It said *Third Grade Talent Show.* "Class, the week is almost over. We only have one more week before the show!"

Cody looked up from his science log. He was drawing some extra pictures of Joe. Joe was getting bigger and bigger and bigger.

"You know that I want everyone to participate," Ms. Harvey began, "but some of you have not told me your talent yet." She looked right at Cody. He blinked. "I will need to know what everyone is going to do for the show before the end of the day tomorrow," Ms. Harvey said.

All morning Cody tried to think of a talent. He had once seen a stand-up comic tell funny jokes on TV.

Then Cody remembered all the jokes in his father's birthday cards. Maybe *he* could tell jokes.

That could be his talent.

"Did you decide?" Chip asked Cody later as they walked to the cafeteria.

"I'm going to be a stand-up comic." Cody smiled confidently. He liked the way that sounded.

"Cool," Chip said. "Tell me a joke."

Cody sighed. "I can't think of any right now," he said.

"I think you need jokes to be a stand-up comic," said Chip.

Cody thought about jokes all through lunch. He couldn't think of a single one.

After lunch he went to the library instead of going outside. He had needed a how-to book once when he was trying to learn how to skate. Surely there would be a book in the media center that would give him some tips on how to be a stand-up comic.

He found a lot of joke books.

1001 Elephant Jokes.

He read one.

What time is it when an elephant sits on a fence?

Time to get a new fence.

He read another one:

How do you keep an elephant from charging?

Take away his credit card.

Those were dumb.

He found a book of knock-knock jokes.

Knock, knock.

Who's there?

Little old lady.

Little old lady who?

I didn't know you could yodel!

Funny. But you needed two people to tell a knock-knock joke.

Then he saw it. *1001 Insults*

He remembered his mother laughing at the birthday cards. The jokes in the book were just like the ones on the cards. They would be a big hit.

He took out a pencil and copied down some jokes. Then he wrote down a few that he remembered from his dad's birthday cards.

When he got back to class everyone was talking at once. Chip turned around in his desk.

"Ms. Harvey is going to let us practice our acts. You get any jokes?"

Cody nodded. He held up the piece of paper and smiled.

"Who wants to go first?" Ms. Harvey asked.

Cody's hand shot up.

"Okay, Cody." Ms. Harvey turned to the class and cleared her throat.

"Introducing," she said as she waved her arm in his direction, "Cody Michaels."

He stood in front of the class with his jokes.

He looked at the paper and took a deep breath.

"Angel is *sooooo* skinny," he said.

"If she sticks out her tongue and turns sideways, people think she's a zipper."

Everyone laughed—everyone except for Angel. She frowned and crossed her arms. Cody loved the sound of the laughter. He tried another one.

"Doug is *soo* dumb, it takes him ten minutes to cook Minute Rice."

Doug stopped laughing and frowned.

Ms. Harvey's mouth was in a tight line. "Cody . . ." she began.

Then Cody remembered the jokes on his father's cards, the ones that had made his mother laugh. They were about being old, but there wasn't anyone in his class who was old except. . . . He looked at Ms. Harvey.

She had a good sense of humor. She would think the jokes were funny. He had to do something—she didn't look very happy right now.

"Ms. Harvey is *soo* old," he said. "Even her wrinkles have wrinkles."

Ms. Harvey's forehead became so wrinkled that for a moment the joke came true—her wrinkles *did* have wrinkles. Then the wrinkles seemed to blur as she moved toward him with great speed.

One minute he was in front of the class, the next minute he was in the hall.

Maybe Ms. Harvey didn't have such a good sense of humor after all. Cody ruled out being a stand-up comic.

My Science Log: The Life of Joe

Day Four:
Life is going well for Joe. Caterpillars do not talk. Silence can be wise.

Chapter 7

That's All, Folks!

Chip was waiting for him the next morning when he arrived at school. "Did you decide what you're going to do for the show?" he asked Cody.

Cody shook his head. "Not yet," he said.

"My countreee, 'tis of theeee!" P.J. sang out from the window of the school bus as it pulled up in front of the school.

"Show off," Chip called out. Holly got off the bus with a large camera case.

She stopped and rested the case on the sidewalk. "How's the video going?" Cody asked her.

"Great," she answered. "I'm going to tape Coach Barns doing the Hokey Pokey."

"Ewwww," Chip said. "I didn't know anyone over twelve could do the Hokey Pokey."

Holly wrinkled her nose and laughed. Cody looked at her and sighed. There was something so cool about a girl who wrinkled her nose when she laughed. He wished that *he* could make her laugh. Should he lower himself to do something silly for the talent show like the Hokey Pokey?

"What are you guys doing for the show?" Holly asked.

"They're doing impersonations of trees," said P.J. as she walked up the steps to school. "They're saps!"

"Ha ha," said Cody. "Why don't you do an impersonation of a tree and leave."

"I can do impersonations," said Chip.

"Do one," said Cody.

"Beep ba beep babeep. That's all, folks!" Chip said in a Porky Pig voice.

"Hey, that's pretty good," Holly said. "Do another."

"I taut I taw a putty tat."

Two other kids stopped to listen.

"Sylvester!" P.J. said.

Cody walked toward the school building alone. Somewhere along the way he must have been left behind in the talent department.

He heard the kids in the crowd around Chip laughing at another impersonation.

Cody tried to think of a time when kids had gathered around him like that.

Then he remembered that in kindergarten he had been the only one who could tie his shoe.

"First you make the twee," he had said as he pulled the lace up into a loop. "Then the bunny goes awound the twee"—he had taken the other lace around the loop—"and into his wittle hole."

For the whole year all the other kids had

come to him when their shoes were untied. Cody sighed. He had never again felt as important as he had when all those kids had lined up to see him make the bunny go awound the twee.

He could imagine it in the talent show.

Cody Michaels will now tie his shoe.

He would step up on the stage.

"Make the twee. The bunny goes awound the twee and into the wittle hole."

Some things are more impressive when you're five.

He desperately tried to remember any other talents that might have made him stand out in the past.

There was the time he had won a prize for collecting the most Campbell's soup labels. He was pretty good at getting the labels off the can.

Cody Michaels will now remove a Campbell's soup label.

That wouldn't be very impressive.

He was great at computer games. He imagined himself playing a computer game on the stage.

Cody Michaels will now zap an alien.

That wasn't the right kind of talent for the show. It was hopeless.

He walked into the classroom with his head down. "Ms. Harvey," he said. "I don't think I want to do an act for the talent show."

"Oh?" She looked up from the papers on her desk.

"Yeah," he said. "I don't think I'll feel like it." He couldn't admit that he didn't have a talent.

"I'm too shy," he said instead.

"Well." She thought for a moment. "I really want everyone to participate." Then she smiled. "I have an idea," she said. "If you don't want to do anything else, you can hold up the signs for each act."

Cody nodded. He took his seat as the other kids came into the room.

Chip stopped by his desk. "I decided not to play the trumpet," he said in a Donald Duck voice. "I'm going to do impersonations instead."

Cody sunk down into his seat. Chip had *two* talents!

"Hey," Holly called out from the back of the room. "Look at the caterpillars! They're hanging upside down." Everyone ran back to look at the little jars. Joe was very still and was hanging upside down from the top of the jar. Even Joe had a talent. Cody walked back to his desk.

He suddenly remembered the name for the stand that holds signs . . . an easel.

That was his talent. Some kids were singers, some trumpet players, some cartoon-character impersonators, and others . . .

Cody Michaels will now be an easel.

It was worse than no talent at all.

My Science Log: The Life of Joe

Day Five:
Joe is hanging upside down. Show off.

Chapter 8

Unlike Cody

Ms. Harvey was excited on Monday morning. "Today we'll go to the stage and practice for the talent show," she said. "Friday is the big night!"

The class lined up and went to the auditorium. Some carried props and others carried instruments. Everyone was laughing and talking at once—everyone except Cody. The weekend had passed and he was still talentless.

As soon as they walked in, Cody noticed the big light in the back of the room. The spotlight.

"Good news," Ms. Harvey said. "We've borrowed a spotlight from the middle school!"

"Cool," Chip said. "I've never been in a spotlight before."

"Me either," Cody said.

"Okay," Ms. Harvey said. "Let's all sit in the audience and we'll practice our acts one at a time. Doug, you're first."

Doug carried a shopping bag and a small folding table up to the stage. He quickly put up the table and put his magic things out on it.

The other kids sat down and watched.

"Friday night we'll have everything ready ahead of time," Ms. Harvey said.

Doug pulled a long black cape out of the bag and tied it around his neck.

P.J. poked Cody in the back. "Doug's a great magician," she said. "Unlike Cody."

Cody sunk lower in his seat. Everyone must know now that he didn't have a talent.

If only he could be a magician. He would wear a long black cape and top hat. Behind him on the stage would be a large box.

"*I need a volunteer from the audience*," he imagined himself saying.

Everyone waved their hands wildly. Everyone wanted to be chosen. Cody knew exactly who to choose.

"*P.J.*," he said. He opened the large box.

P.J. walked proudly to the stage.

She stepped into the box.

Cody closed the box. He took out a magic wand and waved it once.

He waved it twice. He waved it three times. Poof! Smoke billowed out from the box. He opened it and P.J. was gone!

The ultimate vanishing act.

He looked back at P.J. She stuck out her tongue. P.J. was still there.

"Cody," Ms. Harvey called from the stage. "Come on up here. I'll show you where to stand."

"What's he going to do?" Edens whispered.

"I don't know," Chip said.

"*Cody's* going to *do* something," P.J. said.

"I hope he's not going to tell more jokes," Angel said.

Cody walked slowly up to the stage. "Right here," Ms. Harvey said. She pointed to a spot on the side of the stage.

"We don't have the posters yet," she said. "So you'll have to pretend. When I say 'introducing Angel Miller,' then you put up the poster that reads *Angel Miller.* Got it?"

"Got it," Cody echoed.

He stared out sadly at the metal spotlight.

He could hear someone snicker.

On stage Doug was waving a magic wand over a glass of milk. He wished that Doug could wave the wand over him.

Later, when they returned to the room, Holly called, "Hey! Joe's gone." Everyone ran to the table and looked at the jars. Where Joe had been hanging was a green chrysalis. He had disappeared.

My Science Log: The Life of Joe

chrysalis

Jar

Day Eight
Joe is gone. Lucky guy.

Chapter 9

Whoo! Whoa! Wheeee!

After school, Cody lay on his bed with his blanket pulled up over his head. It was dark under the blanket, and he closed his eyes and listened to the sounds of the house.

He could hear his mother downstairs making dinner. Then the doorbell rang, and he heard his mother answer the door.

"Well," she said in the voice that she always used for friends. "Hello, Holly."

Holly!

Holly had come to see him! The blanket flew into the air. He stood up quickly and smoothed his hair. He checked his breath and his zipper. He studied his T-shirt for stains.

"Paul!" his mother called. Cody stopped. She was not calling to *him,* she was calling to his *dad.*

Cody picked up the blanket and wrapped it around his shoulders like a shawl.

He walked down the steps. "Hi, Holly," he said. His voice cracked a little.

"Hi, Cody," she said. "What's the blanket for?"

"Just kind of cold," he said.

"Oh Cody," his mother said. "Holly's making a film about weird adult talents for the talent show at school." Just then, Cody's father walked in.

"Hello, Mr. Michaels," Holly said. "I was just telling Mrs. Michaels that I'm making a video of weird adult talents. Do you have any weird talents?"

"What do you have so far?" Cody's mother asked.

"Mr. Marcini sang 'Happy Birthday' in Italian, Mr. Douglas ate a jelly doughnut in one bite, and Mrs. Douglas did Morse code with her eyebrows."

Cody's father laughed. He thought for a few seconds. "Do we still have that old pogo stick?" he asked.

"Hon-ey," his mother said in a worried voice. "Not that old thing."

Cody covered his eyes. Not the pogo stick. But before he could stop them they were in the garage. His father was going through a tangle of shovels and rakes. "I know it's here somewhere."

"Don't you think you're a little old for that?" Cody asked.

"Old!" His father frowned.

Cody's mother pressed her finger to her lips.

"Old! Old is in the eye of the beholder. I'll show you who's too old. Ah ha!"

He pulled out a rusty pole with a handle on the top. "Here it is!"

"Great," Holly said. "Let's go out in front of the house where there's more light."

They walked out to the driveway. Cody's dad stood behind the stick for a moment.

"Careful, Paul," Cody's mother said. "Don't hurt yourself."

Cody's dad put one foot on the pogo stick and leaned forward. "Are you ready?" he asked Holly. She nodded. The video camera was pressed to her eye. It was pointed right at his dad.

Two kids from across the street joined them. A car slowed down. The people in the car rolled down the window and watched.

"Here we go!" When he said "go," he jumped up on the pogo stick and began to bounce.

"Whoo! Whoa! Wheee!"

He bounced to the right.

The crowd moved to the right.

He bounced to the left.

The crowd moved to the left.

He bounced to the edge of the driveway. The crowd moved with him.

His father bounced twice at the edge of the

rose bed. "Watch out for the roses!" Cody's mother called.

"Whoo! Whoa! Wheeee!" he yelled.

He careened away from the roses and bounced toward the recycle bin. Then he bounced directly into the bin. Cans flew in all directions, and Cody's father seemed to fly into the air with them, in slow motion. The pogo stick flew up with them. Then everything hit the ground.

Cody's father was lying on his back, not moving.

Holly took the camera away from her eye. "Is he okay?"

"Paul, Paul." His mother patted his father's face.

"Uuuuuh," he said finally. "I'm okay." He sat up slowly.

Cody was frozen to one spot of the driveway. "You didn't get that, did you?" he asked Holly.

Holly nodded. "It was great," she said. "This is the worst one yet."

She put the cap over the camera lens. "Thanks, Mr. Michaels," she said.

He waved weakly from the pile of cans.

"Bye, Cody," Holly said. "I've got to get over to Chip's house. His mother's going to do the Macarena."

Cody watched Holly hurry down the street. The whole event had been like a natural disaster. One minute he had been in his room quietly minding his own business, and the next he had been in the driveway watching his dad flying through the air with thirty cans. And it had been filmed for the whole school to see.

Cody pulled the blanket completely over his head and felt his way into the house and upstairs to his bedroom.

Chapter 10

A Thousand Words

"Go cheer your father up," Cody's mother said. She poked the blanket. Cody peeked out from under it.

He hated it when people said things like that. Like when his teacher gave them a writing assignment and said, "make it interesting." But she never said exactly how to do that. Or when his coach said, "Win one for the Gipper." What was a Gipper? Cody always imagined that they were winning the game for a giant fish.

"Come on," she said. "You've been up here napping too long."

Cody sat up and gathered his blanket around himself. He walked downstairs to where his father was lying on the sofa with a Baggie full of ice on his knee.

"You okay, Dad?" Cody sat down on the chair beside the sofa. His father's eyes were closed.

"Dad?"

No answer.

Cody sat for a minute. He tried to think of something encouraging to say, but he could only think of the pogo stick and the flying cans and the sound of the crunch that the cans made when his dad jumped into the bin. How embarrassing.

He couldn't think of much to say to cheer his dad up. "Dad," he said finally. "That was some fall."

No answer.

"I didn't know a man your age could jump so high."

His dad moaned. It was the wrong thing to say.

"You missed the roses," he said hopefully.

"Uuuuuh."

"I mean—"

"I'm too old," his father interrupted. "Your mother was right. I'm just too old for anything anymore." He pointed to the birthday cards on the mantel, the ones that said *Too bad you're not wine or cheese* and *Your wrinkles have wrinkles.*

"They're right," he said.

Cody bit his lip. He wanted to tell his father that dads were supposed to be old. He wanted to tell him that it was okay, but he couldn't think of how to say the words. He understood how his dad felt. The sound in his dad's voice reminded him of the way he felt about the talent show. Kind of hopeless.

What could he do to cheer his dad up? He thought for a while in silence. He looked at the birthday cards lined up on the mantel again. Then he had an idea.

Cody went up to his room and took out his art supplies and began to draw a card of his own.

When it was done, he took it downstairs.

His dad was still on the sofa with his eyes closed.

"Dad?"

"Huh."

"I made you a card."

"I don't think I can take another card."

"You'll like this one."

His father opened his eyes and took it.

"What's this?" His father opened the card.

Cody sat down. "I drew a timeline of your life." He pointed to the drawings inside the card. "That's when you were born." There was a picture of a baby. "That's when you broke your wrist. That's when you got your first job at the Pizza Inn. That's when you got married." There was a small picture of a bride and groom that looked like Cody's mom and dad. "That's when you got your job at the bank. That's when we moved from Topeka."

"This is great work, Cody. What's this?"

The end of the line was blank. Just a long line going on and on to the end of the paper.

His father ran his finger along the line.

"That's your future," Cody said. "We can fill it in as you go along."

His father smiled. "Sometimes, Cody, you know just what to say."

"I do?"

His father nodded. "Bring me all those cards." Cody went to the mantel and picked up all the birthday cards. His dad tossed them into the trash can beside the sofa.

"Now put that one up." Cody put his card on the mantle.

"A picture is worth a thousand words," his dad said.

Cody thought about how that was true. A picture could tell a story. A picture could hurt someone's feelings or make someone feel better.

"That groom really looks like me."

Cody smiled. "It does?"

"Yes. And this picture of your mother. I don't know how you did it but it looks like her, too. You are very talented," his dad said.

"I have a talent?" Cody asked. "Wait a minute. I have a *talent.*" He felt good inside. Like he was complete. He took his blanket off from around his shoulders and tucked it around his father's hurt leg.

He noticed that his dad's smile lines were crinkled and when he touched the corner of his own eye, he felt that it was crinkling too.

My Science Log: The Life of Joe

Day Nine:
Joe must be working on something great in there.

Day Ten:
I bet Joe will be excited when it's time to come out of the cocoon.

Day Eleven:
Joe looks <u>almost</u> ready.

Day Twelve:
Come out, Joe. You're going to be beautiful!

Chapter 11

The Show

Behind the curtain on stage, everyone was nervous. P.J. was warming up her voice. La la la LA la la la. She sang up and down the scale.

Cody peeked out the crack between the curtains. He could see all the families waiting for the show to begin.

P.J.'s mother and father were in the front row. They looked excited. Doug's grandmother and Holly's parents all looked very eager.

"Let's see." Chip peeked out too.

"Not too wide," Cody warned. "Or they'll see us."

Cody spotted his mother and father sitting about three rows back. His mother waved.

"It's time," Ms. Harvey said.

Cody took a deep breath. There were a lot of people out there.

He stepped out from between the curtains and onto the stage. He moved to the side where the large easel and a pile of signs awaited him. Everyone applauded, then became very quiet. Cody's heart was racing. His palms were sweaty. The spotlight was traveling all around the room like a searchlight looking for someone.

He could see Ms. Harvey standing on the other side of the stage behind a microphone. She smiled at him and gave him the thumbs-up sign. He reached down and gripped the top of the first sign.

The spotlight found Ms. Harvey. "Welcome to the third-grade talent show!" she said. Everyone clapped and cheered. Cody's fingers tightened on the sign.

"Our first act tonight," Ms. Harvey said in

a very dramatic voice, "will be P.J. Donaldson singing 'America, the Beautiful.' "

Ms. Harvey nodded in Cody's direction. "And our wonderful posters tonight were made by our own talented Cody Michaels." The spotlight swung over to his side of the stage.

For a moment, the light was in Cody's eyes and he couldn't see the audience anymore. He couldn't see his parents or Holly's parents—just a bright glare.

He put the sign up on the easel. At the top of the sign he had written "P.J." In the middle of the sign he had drawn a picture of P.J. singing on a stage. There was an American flag waving behind her and fireworks in the sky.

The curtain opened for P.J.'s act and she stepped forward. She looked at the poster and then at Cody and smiled. She liked her picture! Everyone liked the picture. For one wonderful second Cody felt that the talent show was perfect.

70

The spotlight focused on P.J. now instead of him. He realized something then. When the spotlight is on you, you can't see anyone else—and he didn't like that. But he loved the warm glow he had felt when everyone had seen the picture that *he* had drawn.

Everyone's talents were different. From singing to dancing. From the Hokey Pokey to the Macarena. From making a movie to making a poster. Just like his dad had said, everyone has a best thing to share.

As he stood in the dark beside the easel watching P.J. take a bow, his hands gripped the next picture. This one was of Holly with her video camera.

"Our next act will be Holly Wade," Ms. Harvey said. Cody smiled and put Holly's picture on the easel. He couldn't wait to see her in the spotlight.

Chapter 12

Come On, Joe!

"They're coming out!"

The class ran back to the table first thing Monday morning and clustered around the jars.

"Come on, Joe," Holly said, as they watched Joe struggling to get out of his chrysalis.

"Can we help them, Ms. Harvey?" P.J. asked.

"No," Ms. Harvey said. "If they don't get out by themselves, their wings won't be strong enough. They have to do it alone."

"Come on, Joe!" Cody said.

"Come on," Chip echoed.

They watched the chrysalis break open as Joe slowly pulled himself out and stretched his wings.

"He made it!" Cody said. Joe extended his wings and beat them back and forth in the air to dry them.

"After lunch we'll let them fly away," Ms. Harvey said.

Cody watched Joe flapping his new wings. They looked graceful and strong.

"He's beautiful," Holly said. Cody looked at her and sighed. There was something so cool about a girl who liked butterflies.

My Science Log: The Life of Joe

Joe

Jar

Day Fifteen:
Today Joe became a butterfly. You should see him fly. What talent!